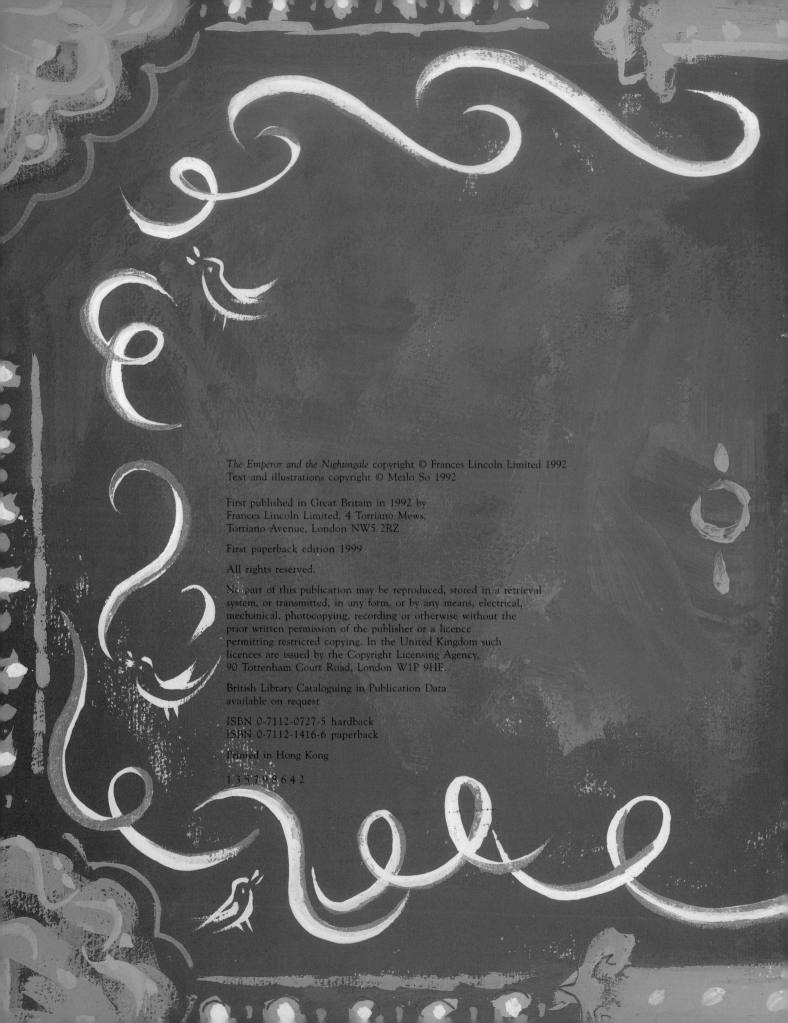

First published in Great Britain in 1992 by
Frances Lincoln Limited, 4 Torriano Mews,
Torriano Avenue, London NW5 2RZ

First paperback edition 1999

British Library Cataloguing in Publication Data
available on request

ISBN 0-7112-0727-5 hardback
ISBN 0-7112-1416-6 paperback

Printed in Hong Kong

1 3 5 7 9 8 6 4 2

Meilo So was born in Hong Kong and first came to the United Kingdom in 1979 to complete her education. After finishing school she studied art in Oxford and Brighton before returning to Hong Kong to embark upon a career as a freelance illustrator. She is now a part-time illustrator with many magazine credits to her name. Her previous titles for Frances Lincoln include *The Monkey and the Panda*, written by Antonia Barber and *Wishbones*, written by Barbara Ker Wilson, which was chosen as one of the Children's Books of the Year 1994.
Meilo lives and works in Hong Kong.

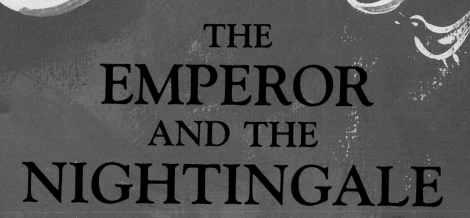

THE
EMPEROR
AND THE
NIGHTINGALE

*Inspired by Hans Christian Andersen's
"The Nightingale"*

Retold and illustrated by
MEILO SO

FRANCES LINCOLN

This story takes place in China, soon after the Emperor's new palace had been completed.

Travellers came from far and wide to marvel at the palace. They praised its beauty and wrote books about it.

When the Emperor read the books, he found this sentence: "The palace is full of wonderful things, but the song of the nightingale is the best of all."

The Emperor had not realised there was such a bird in his palace. He called for his Prime Minister.

"The nightingale must sing for me!" the Emperor said.
The Prime Minister sent soldiers to search everywhere for the nightingale, but they could not find her. Not until the Prime Minister met a little kitchen maid did he solve the puzzle.

"The nightingale sings for me every evening," the little kitchen maid said.

She led the courtiers into the forest and pointed to a tiny grey bird. The bird was not pretty, but her singing was the most beautiful they had ever heard.

That evening, the little nightingale sang for the Emperor. When he heard her song of piercing beauty, tears ran down the Emperor's cheeks. The nightingale was awarded a golden cage and twelve footmen to wait upon her.

She was permitted to fly outside the palace twice daily.

One day, a new toy arrived for the Emperor.
It was a mechanical nightingale. It sang
the same songs as the real bird – very
beautifully – and it was prettier too.

Sometimes the two birds sang together, but it was never a success. The real nightingale sang as the mood took her, while the mechanical one could only sing the notes it had been made to sing.

One afternoon, when the cage had been left open, the real bird flew away without anyone noticing.

The Emperor did not mind. He listened to the mechanical bird instead.

Then, one day, the mechanical nightingale refused to sing.

The royal clockmaker examined it.
"The bird is wearing out," he said.
"From now on it must sing only on special occasions."

As the years went by, the mechanical bird sang less and less, until it could not sing at all.

By now, the Emperor himself was old and worn. He had become very ill.

The Emperor begged the mechanical bird to sing to soothe his pain, but to no avail.

Suddenly he heard a beautiful voice outside the window. It was the real nightingale. She sang of the fierce joy of living and of the beauty that the world conceals under a drab coat.

The Emperor's pain began to ease.

"How can I repay you?" asked the Emperor.

"You have rewarded me already, with the tears that you shed the first time you heard me sing," said the nightingale.

She sang again, and then said, "I was not made to sit on golden perches. Sleep now. When you wake I will come and sing to you of the things that happen in your kingdom, but let it be our secret. For the singing bird flies far and sees things that are hidden from an Emperor's eyes."

The Emperor thanked the nightingale, and sank into a deep, peaceful sleep.

And that was the beginning of the secret friendship between the great Emperor and the little nightingale.

MORE PICTURE BOOKS IN PAPERBACK FROM FRANCES LINCOLN

WISHBONES

Barbara Ker Wilson
Meilo So

Wishbones, magic fishbones that make every dream come true ... From south of the clouds comes this oriental fable, weaving riches and sorrows into the enchanted tale of a golden-eyed fish, a lost slipper and a king's search for his bride.

Suitable for National Curriculum English – Reading, Key Stages 1 and 2
Scottish Guidelines English Language – Reading, Levels B and C

ISBN 0-7112-1415-8 £4.99

THE MONKEY AND THE PANDA

Antonia Barber
Meilo So

Lean, lively Monkey plays naughty tricks and makes the village children laugh.
But in their quieter moments the children prefer the company of fat, friendly Panda.
This original story cleverly combines allegory with fun and will enchant animal lovers everywhere.

Suitable for National Curriculum English – Reading, Key Stages 1 and 2
Scottish Guidelines English Language – Reading, Level C

ISBN 0-7112-1085-3 £4.99

LORD OF THE ANIMALS

Fiona French

Coyote has created the world and its creatures, and now he gathers a council to decide how they will make the being who will rule over them all. This fascinating Native American Miwok myth tells the story of how human beings began.

Suitable for National Curriculum English – Reading, Key Stages 1 and 2
Scottish Guidelines English Language – Reading, Levels A and B

ISBN 0-7112-1348-8 £4.99

Frances Lincoln titles are available from all good bookshops.
Prices are correct at time of publication, but may be subject to change.